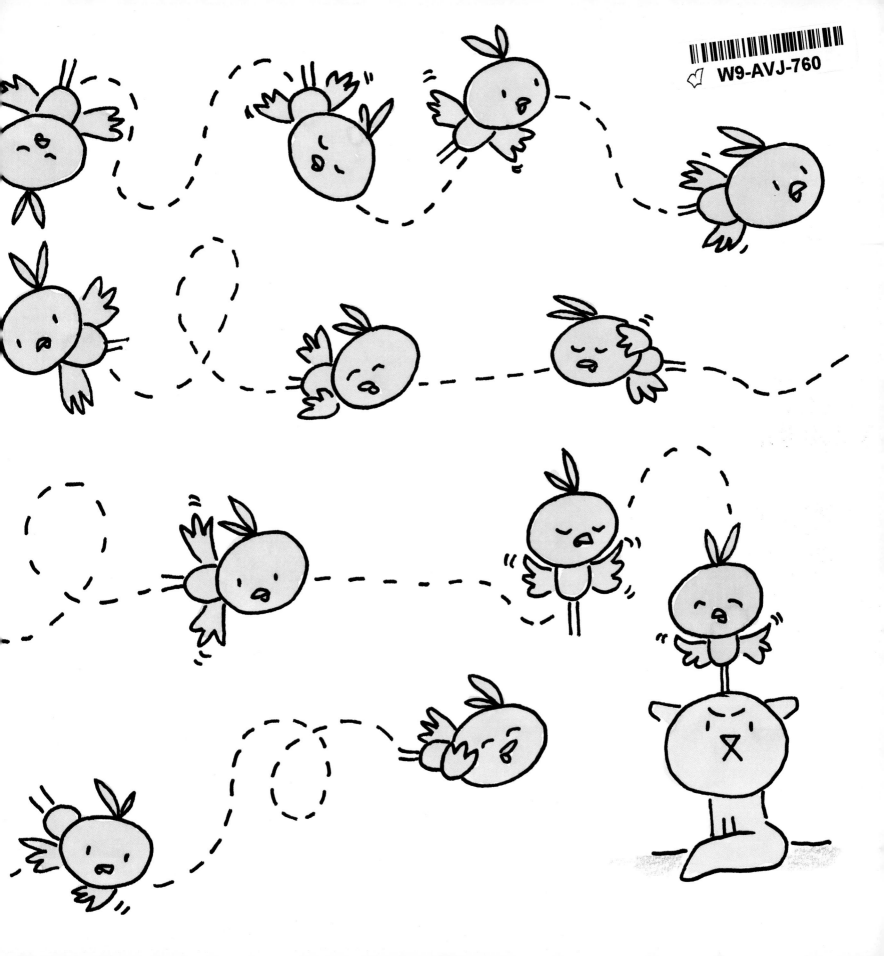

Did You Eat the Parakeet?

Mark Iacolina

Farrar Straus Giroux

New York

For Ally and Tyler—

my best days are always the ones spent with you

Did you eat the parakeet?

He was right there on his tiny seat!

He was singing a tune just an hour ago.

Did you eat him?
I want to know!

Did you eat the parakeet?

Did he become
a tasty treat?

You usually play
so nicely together.

Now all that's left
is this single feather.

Did you eat the parakeet?

Did you laugh
and say *Bon appétit?*

He was such a small and scrawny bird.

To eat him
would be absurd!

THE PARAKEET?

His head?

His beak?

His wings?

His feet?

He was quite
the dashing,
handsome fellow.

Minty green, with a touch of yellow.

You
did *not* eat
the parakeet!

He did NOT become a tasty treat!

You did NOT enjoy a bird buffet,
a budgie *brûlée*, or a feathered flambé!

I'm sorry for getting so carried away.

But wait . . .

. . . I haven't seen the mouse all day!

Farrar Straus Giroux Books for Young Readers
An imprint of Macmillan Publishing Group, LLC
175 Fifth Avenue, New York, NY 10010

Color separations by Bright Arts (H.K.) Ltd.
Printed in China by RR Donnelley Asia Printing Solutions Ltd.,
Dongguan City, Guangdong Province
First edition, 2018

1   3   5   7   9   10   8   6   4   2

mackids.com

Library of Congress Cataloging-in-Publication Data

Names: Iacolina, Mark, author, illustrator.
Title: Did you eat the parakeet? / Mark Iacolina.
Description: First edition. | New York : Margaret Ferguson Books/Farrar
    Straus Giroux, 2018. | Summary: "A little girl can't find her
    parakeet—her kitty must have eaten it! Right? Where else would it have
    gone? It was just here! She shouts, she accuses, and she laments her loss.
    But her cat might be trying to tell her something . . ."—Provided by
    publisher
Identifiers: LCCN 2017013636 | ISBN 9780374305888 (hardcover)
Subjects: | CYAC: Stories in rhyme. | Cats—Fiction. | Parakeets—Fiction. |
    Humorous stories.
Clasification: LCC PZ8.3.I23365 Di 2018 | DDC [E]—dc23
LC record available at https://lccn.loc.gov/2017013636

Our books may be purchased in bulk for promotional, educational, or business use.
Please contact your local bookseller or the Macmillan Corporate
and Premium Sales Department at (800) 221-7945 ext. 5442
or by e-mail at MacmillanSpecialMarkets@macmillan.com.